The Unexpected Treasure

ISBN 978-1-0980-9307-5 (paperback)
ISBN 978-1-0980-9309-9 (hardcover)
ISBN 978-1-0980-9308-2 (digital)

Christian Faith Publishing, Inc.
832 Park Avenue
Meadville, PA 16335
www.christianfaithpublishing.com

Printed in the United States of America

The Unexpected Treasure

Oliver Debayle

An adventurous boy named Brayden lived with his parents in a big blue house. Brayden loved exploring the woods for dinosaur footprints, making friends with garden bugs, and filling his pockets with rocks to add to his collection. Brayden and his dad spent hours playing together and going on lots of exciting adventures.

One morning, Brayden and his dad were reading a book about pirates and buried treasure.

"Hey Dad, I wonder if there is any treasure buried near our house." Brayden said.

"There might be! Should we go search for some?" his dad asked.

"Oh, please, please, please," Brayden replied.

His dad smiled and then asked, "And what would you do with the treasure, Brayden?"

"Well, I would buy a flying car and a pet shark!" Brayden said.

"I love your big imagination, Brayden. But can you think of any other ideas for normal stuff?" his dad asked.

"Hmm…. I'd love a swing set for the backyard," Brayden said, while pointing to the garden through the window.

"Good thinking, Brayden. Let's go find some treasure!" his dad replied.

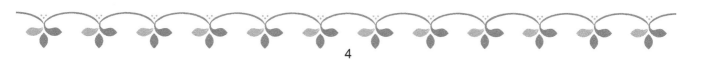

Brayden and his dad climbed way up high into their backyard treehouse to look for places that might have buried treasure. Brayden thought like the pirate from the book. "Pirates like to bury their treasure in sand," he said. He thought of three places with sand: Hugo Park, Uncle Marshall's ranch, and Murphey Beach. "I'm sure an old pirate would bury his treasure there," he said. His dad agreed and they set off to find some treasure.

At Hugo Park, Brayden and his dad dug and dug for treasure. But they couldn't find any. They only found a few children's toys, a dog bone, and a girl's red bow.

Suddenly, Brayden heard a noise—***thump, thump, thump***. It was the sound of children packing sand into buckets to build sandcastles.

Brayden and his dad joined in. They built what turned out to be one of the biggest and silliest sandcastles they'd ever made.

Brayden's dad looked at him with pride and said, "Way to go, Son!" Brayden smiled and said, "Let's keep searching for some treasure, Dad!"

At Uncle Marshall's ranch, Brayden asked to ride Uncle Marshall's biggest and fastest horse, Hercules. While riding, Brayden heard a familiar noise—***thump, thump, thump***. It was the sound of Hercules's hooves hitting the ground. At one point, Brayden let go of the reins to spread his arms wide toward the sky. "I feel like I'm flying!" he said. They made many stops around the ranch to dig for treasure, but they didn't have any luck.

They arrived at Murphey Beach to look for treasure, but the hot sand began to hurt Brayden's feet. Brayden and his dad jumped into the refreshing water to cool off. After playing for some time, they continued looking for some treasure.

15

As they were digging, they heard a familiar noise—***thump, thump, thump***. It was the sound of their shovels hitting something wooden that was buried in the sand.

Brayden's heart began to beat faster. They dug and dug and found…

"It's only a piece of wood! There's no treasure here." Brayden said as he lowered his shoulders and sighed. He then walked to a bench and sat down.

Brayden's dad held him tightly and let Brayden rest his head on his chest. Brayden then heard a familiar noise—***thump, thump, thump***. It was the sound of his dad's heartbeat!

The ***thump, thump, thump*** sound reminded Brayden of all the things he had done that day, like building sandcastles, riding horses, and digging for treasure on the beach. Brayden wasn't so sad anymore; he loved thinking about his adventures with dad.

He looked up at his dad and smiled.

"Are you feeling better?" his dad asked.

Brayden nodded.

"Did you have fun today?" his dad added.

"Yes, I did," Brayden replied.

His dad held Brayden a little tighter, kissed his forehead, and said, "You are my treasure, Brayden."

"And you're my treasure too, Dad," Brayden said.

"Looks like we had our treasure all along," his dad replied.

A few days later, Brayden came home from school and his dad waved at him.

"Come outside to the backyard, Brayden. I have a surprise for you," his dad said.

When Brayden got there, he noticed something new. It was the swing set that he had wanted! Brayden and his dad ran over and jumped on the swings. They played on the swing set for hours and didn't stop swinging until the sun set behind them.

CPSIA information can be obtained
at www.ICGtesting.com
Printed in the USA
BVHW050940221121
622229BV00015B/546